Fast Friends

A Tail and Tongue Tale

By Lisa Horstman

WINNER OF THE FIRST DR. SEUSS PICTURE BOOK AWARD

Alfred A. Knopf New York

For Mom and Dad, who always set a good example; and for Dave

THIS IS A BORZOI BOOK PUBLISHED BY ALFRED A. KNOPF, INC.

Text and illustrations copyright © 1994 by Lisa Horstman

All rights reserved under International and Pan-American Copyright Conventions. Published in the United States of America by Alfred A. Knopf, Inc., New York, and simultaneously in Canada by Random House of Canada Limited, Toronto. Distributed by Random House, Inc., New York.

Library of Congress Cataloging-in-Publication Data
Horstman, Lisa
Fast friends : a tail and tongue tale / written and illustrated by Lisa Horstman.
p.   cm.
Summary: A cow and a chameleon move to the big city and become roommates until their considerable differences threaten to ruin their friendship.
ISBN 0-679-85404-5 (trade) ISBN 0-679-95404-X (lib. bdg.)
[1. Cows—Fiction. 2. Chameleons—Fiction. 3. Friendship—Fiction.]
I. Title.
PZ7.H7914Fas   1994   [E]—dc20   93-28630

Manufactured in the United States of America
10 9 8 7 6 5 4 3 2 1

Do you have a friend who's completely different from you? It happens. Maybe you're quiet and your friend is noisy. Or maybe you're short and your friend is as tall as a tree. Does this sound like you? If it does, have I got a story for you. . . .

One sunny September morning, a cow named Blueberry Sprig left his small farm to make his way in the world.

As he lumbered along, a fly landed on his back. "That's a nuisance," he exclaimed, and with a loud THWAKK! his tail expertly flicked it off.

SLURP! "Why, yes, indeed it must be." A dapper chameleon passing by shot out his long tongue, caught the bug, and gobbled it up.

"Who are you?" asked Blueberry Sprig, filled with admiration.

"My name is Smithfield, and I'm off to become a chef for the richest woman in town. I am the best chef there is; otherwise she never would have chosen me," he stated.

Blueberry's eyes beheld this majestic creature. He did not doubt him one iota.

"I," mooed Blueberry, "hope to work for the city paper as their cow-about-town."

"Oh, indeed?" rasped Smithfield. "Well, then, let's be practical and travel together."

Happy to have such an elegant companion on the long journey, the cow agreed.

Off they plodded, kerTHUNK, kerTHUNK, till at last they reached the twinkling skyscrapers of the city.

Smithfield examined the sight before him. Finally he said, "Mr. Blueberry Sprig, it seems very practical for us to be roommates."

"What a fine idea!" mooed Blueberry, flattered by the lizard's offer.

So life in the city began for Smithfield and Blueberry Sprig.
Blueberry got a job working on *The City Pen* and was quite happy.
Everyone was always nice to him because they knew he might write
about them.

Smithfield was a very fine chef for the richest woman in town, who was often mentioned in Blueberry's column.

And the two became fast friends. Sometimes after a long day, they would go out for a stroll together.

Or sometimes Smithfield would cook a huge gourmet meal for their friends.

Or sometimes they would simply sit by the fireplace
reading their favorite books.

But their greatest pleasure was bug-thwakking. "That's a nuisance,"
Blueberry would always say before a particularly satisfying THWAKK.
SLURP! "Why, yes, indeed it must be," Smithfield always replied.

Still, life in the small, cramped house was not ideal. Blueberry, being a cow, took up lots of space. And he wasn't very tidy.

Smithfield, on the other hand, was *extremely* tidy. He constantly followed Blueberry around, saying things like "Can't you pick up your dirty socks?" . . . "And for heaven's sake, these hoofprints are ruining the floor! I just waxed!" Nag, nag, nag.

Poor Blueberry tried to be neat. He was very careful to wash his dirty dishes—sometimes.

And make his bed—when he remembered.

And do his laundry—when Smithfield reminded him.

But old habits are hard to break.

One day, Blueberry returned from a society tea exhausted. He'd been on his hooves all day, and the only thing he could think of was a rest in the big, soft chair by the sunny window. As he eased himself down, first an "Aaaah!" but then an "Ouch!" and finally a "Great horny toads!" pierced the air.

"MmmmMMMOOOO!" shrieked Blueberry, startled.

He jumped up. On the chair's seat was Smithfield, glaring up at him with pure anger on his face. He had been sunning himself and, being a chameleon, had blended right in with the flowered fabric.

"You . . . you . . . you . . . cow! You sat on me! Can't you ever watch what you're doing?" he screamed. "Well, I can't take this another minute!" And without further ado, he stomped into his room, packed his bags, and left.

Blueberry Sprig slumped to the floor. His best friend was gone. What would he do? How would he ever survive?

Days passed. Smithfield stayed with an old acquaintance, a prairie dog who liked to eat banana chips in the middle of the night. CRRRRUNCH! *Smack, smack*. CRRRRUNCH! *Smack, smack*. It drove Smithfield into a frenzy, but his pride kept him put.

Blueberry Sprig was lonely in the little house. His cow-about-town job didn't seem to be much fun anymore. In fact, *nothing* seemed much fun.

The cow took to going on long, solitary walks through
the park. One twilit evening, as he lumbered along, a fly
landed on his back. "That's a nuisance," he exclaimed, and
with a loud THWAKK! his tail expertly flicked it off.

SLURP! "Why, yes, indeed it must be." There was Smithfield,
who shot out his long tongue, caught the bug, and gobbled it up.

The two friends eyed each other carefully. "Oh, Smithfield," Blueberry cried, "I miss you! Please come back to the house and be my roommate again."

"Well, I don't know," said Smithfield slowly. But suddenly his appetite—and satisfying it—seemed very important. And besides, maybe he did miss Blueberry just a little.

Smithfield jumped down to the grass and said, "Despite your piggish ways, your ability to attract bugs is unusual, and your method of catching them *is* practical. I admire that." He paused. "I suppose I could be more tolerant of your sloppiness. After all, you *are* a cow."

"Well, I admire your very tidy disposal of bugs. I'll try to be neater," promised Blueberry Sprig.

And so life began again for Smithfield
and Blueberry Sprig. Sometimes
Blueberry would accidentally leave
a wet towel on the bathroom floor
after his bath.

Once in a while, Smithfield would complain
about toast crumbs in the butter dish.

But the bug-catching system prevailed, and all were happy with the arrangement.

Except, of course, the bugs.